The Festival of Bones
El Festival de las Calaveras

THE LITTLE-BITTY BOOK FOR THE DAY OF THE DEAD

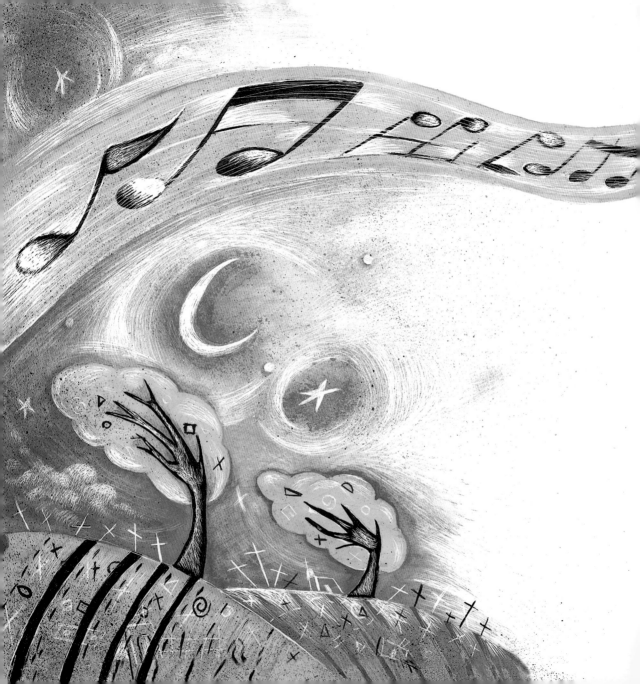

THE LITTLE-BITTY BOOK
FOR THE DAY OF THE DEAD

The Festival of Bones
El Festival de las Calaveras

LUIS SAN VICENTE

TRANSLATION BY
John William Byrd & Bobby Byrd

CINCO PUNTOS PRESS • EL PASO, TEXAS

EL PASO, TEXAS

Cover & book design by
Vicki Trego Hill of El Paso, Texas.

*Many thanks to Marta Llorens of Alfaguara,
Ben Sáenz for his generous collaboration and
Susannah Mississippi Byrd for discovering
this book in the first place.*

Originally published in Mexico in 1999 as *El Festival de las Calaveras* by Alfaguara, an imprint of Grupo Santillana. Copyright text © 1999, Luis San Vicente. Copyright illustrations © 1999, Luis San Vicente.

Festival of the Bones / El Festival de las Calaveras.

FIRST EDITION
10   9   8   7   6

Library of Congress Cataloging-in-Publication Data
San Vicente, Luis. [Festival de las Calaveras. English]
Festival of the bones = El festival de las calaveras : the little-bitty book for the day of the dead / written and illustrated by Luis San Vicente.—1st ed.   p. cm.
"Originally published in Mexico as El Festival de las calaveras." Summary: Describes the Day of the Dead, or el Día de los Muertos, a holiday celebrated in Mexico from October 31 to November 2.
ISBN-13: 978-0-938317-67-8
ISBN-10: 0-938317-67-9 (HC)
1. All Souls' Day—Mexico—Juvenile literature.
2. Mexico—Social life and customs—Juvenile literature. [1. All Souls' Day—Mexico. 2. Holidays—Mexico.
3. Mexico—Social life and customs. 4. Spanish language materials—Bilingual.] I. Title.
GT4995.A4 S2513 2002 394.266—dc21   2002009764

Printed in Hong Kong by Morris Printing

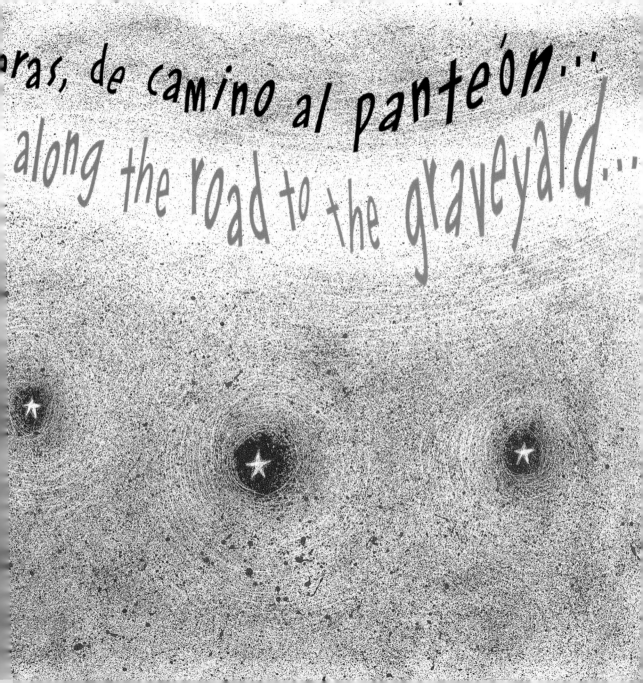

...ras, de camino al panteón..."

...along the road to the graveyard..."

THEY ARE COMING and they are going
And you see them passing by.
They are walking over here,
They are walking over there…
These are the dead.
How happy they are!

VAN y vienen
Y las ves pasar.
Andan por ahí,
Andan por allá…
Son las calaveras
Que felices están.

HEY, I'm flying!
Hey, I'm flying!
The festival is so far away...
The Day of the Dead is today.

¡VOY que vuelo!
¡Voy que vuelo!
Ahí a lo lejos se ve el festejo...
Hoy es Día de muertos.

THEY'RE COMING and they're going
And you see them passing by.
They're dancing over here,
They're chatting over there...
It's their day
And they're going to have a good time.

VAN y vienen
Y las ves pasar.
Bailan por ahí,
Platican por allá...
Es su día
Y van a festejar.

PASCUAL'S SKELETON sings a song
Without any pain or dread
Although half a leg is really gone
Still a flower sits upon his head.

LA CALACA PASCUALA canta
Sin pena ni temor
Aunque le falte una pata
Y en el sombrero lleve una flor.

atole y pan!
atole & bread!

CALAVERAS

¡Es la . . . ofrenda
It's the . . . offering
&
dinner
is served!
y
servida
está!

IN THE CEMETERY

The kids are asking for the baby skeleton,
With her scary mask
And her box with the little candle.

EN EL CAMPOSANTO

Los niños piden calaverita
Con su máscara de espanto
Y su caja con velita.

GIDDYUP! Giddyup!
Oh, they want to catch me.
To that ugly skeleton…
They want to marry me.

¡ARRE, arre!
Que me quieren alcanzar.
Con esa calaca fea…
Me quieren desposar.

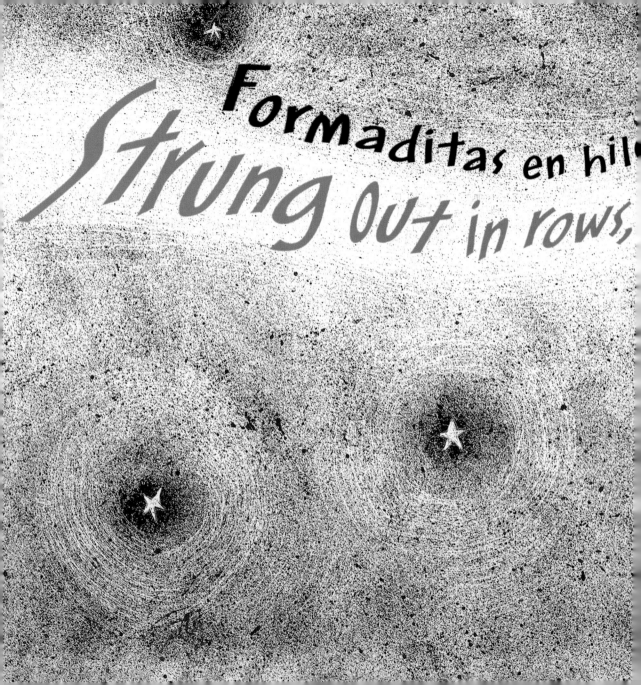

Formaditas en hil[e]

Strung out in rows,

The Day of the Dead

The Day of the Dead is an ancient Aztec celebration of death, the bitter-sweet companion to life. Over hundreds of years, the Day of the Dead has become a part of the Catholic tradition in Mexico. This holiday—which actually lasts two nights and three days—is a time when people remember family and friends who have died. Many believe that the dead return home and visit loved ones, feast on their favorite foods and listen to their favorite music. In their homes, the family honors and celebrates their deceased with ofrendas or offerings. They give thanks for the lives of the people they loved. During the Day of the Dead, people also recognize the importance of life itself.

People in Mexico celebrate the Day of the Dead from October 31 to November 2. Beginning on the night of October 31 and continuing through November 1, they remember the lives of children who have died. They remember the lives of adults who have died

beginning on the night of November 1 and continuing
on through November 2.

How Can You Celebrate the Day of the Dead?

If you're lucky enough to be in Mexico
during the festivities for el Día de los muertos, make
sure you visit the local cemetery. Many families visit the graves of
their loved ones. They clean the graves up, making sure the grass is
trimmed or the surrounding ground is swept, that fresh paint is
applied where it's needed and that every part of the gravesite is
renewed and refreshed. Then they decorate the grave itself with
flowers. Often families and friends will make themselves comfortable
on blankets or in chairs and have a picnic at the gravesite, eating the
favorite foods of the person who has died and telling stories about
that person's life. Sometimes the visitors stay all up night, enjoying
good times with their relatives, both the living and the dead.

One of the most common ways to celebrate the Day of the Dead
in Mexico is to build an altar. Some people build the altar at the grave
and some build it in their living room or in their backyard. But no
matter where the altar is built, it is always something special that the
dead person will be sure to enjoy.

In other places outside of Mexico, people freely borrow elements of the Day of the Dead to create their own traditions. You can, too! Just remember, though: even though you honor and remember the dead on the Day of the Dead, it is a happy and social occasion. It's a party, not a funeral.

How to Build an Altar

There are many ways to build and decorate an altar. You can use your imagination. Ask yourself, *Whose life would I like to remember?* (If you want, you can celebrate the lives of more than one person.) *What did this person love when he or she was alive? What food or drink? What kind of flowers? What sort of perfume? What favorite things did he or she do? What games?*

When you have thought about the person who died, you can make your altar as personal as you want. Let the altar bring to mind all the things that person liked when he or she was alive.

First, find a table or cardboard box that you can decorate. Make sure you ask your parents or teacher if you can use that table or cardboard box for at least three days.

Second, find a picture of the person whose life you want to celebrate. Put that picture on the altar—maybe in the center— where everyone will see it. Many families also put a cross or a picture of a favorite saint near or beside the picture of the person who has died.

Third, decorate the table. Some of the items people decorate their altars with are candles, pretty paper called "papel picado," candy skulls, food like pan de muerto (bread of the dead), and special drinks like hot chocolate or a fruit drink.

If you use candles, make sure your teacher or parents help you light them. You can buy papel picado, candy skulls, and pan de muerto at stores that specialize in Mexican crafts or on the Internet, but you can make your own if you want. We've provided recipes for pan de muerto and candy skulls on the pages that follow.

For papel picado, you need brightly colored tissue paper, scissors and a fun imagination. Fold the paper up, doubling it at least four times. Then take your scissors and cut designs into the edges of the folds. Maybe cut off some corners here and there. Then unfold the paper once and cut some more designs. Do it again and again until you have unfolded the paper completely. Look what you have created! ¡Un papel picado! Make as many as you want. Take your time and enjoy yourself. If you want to learn more about papel picado, we suggest you read *Making Magic Windows: Creating Cut-Paper Art* by Carmen Lomas Garza.

You can also include items that show the things that the person did when they were alive. For example, maybe the person you loved was a doctor. You can include a stethoscope on the table. Maybe he

or she loved to garden—you can include a packet of seeds or some gardening gloves.

When you decorate, don't forget the flowers! Many people like to use marigolds and chrysanthemums for altars dedicated to adults, and baby's breath or white orchids for altars dedicated to babies. Think about what flowers that person liked and include those on the altar.

Last, but not least, you can offer your loved one a gift that you think would make them happy—a pretty bracelet, a book they always liked, or a crazy hat.

How to Make Pan de Muerto

Pan de Muerto is a sweet bread shaped like an oval, although it can also be shaped like a person or an animal or even a bone!

Ingredients:
2 packets of dry yeast
1½ cups of flour
1 tablespoon of anise seed
½ cup of sugar
1 teaspoon of salt
½ cup of milk
½ cup of water

½ cup of butter
4 eggs
3 – 4½ cups of flour

Preparation: Mix all dry ingredients together except the 3 – 4½ cups of flour. Heat, but don't boil, the milk, water, and butter in a small pan and then add it to the dry mixture. Beat well.

Add the eggs and 1½ cups of the additional flour to this mixture. Beat well. Slowly mix in the rest of the flour, a little at a time.

Flour a cutting board. Knead the mixture on the cutting board for 9 – 10 minutes. Put the dough in a greased bowl and allow it to rise until it has doubled in size (about 1 to 1½ hours at sea level). Punch the dough down and shape it however you want—as a person, animal, bone, or in an oval shape. Let it rise for another hour.

Bake at 350° F (175° C) for about 40 minutes. After baking, sprinkle it with colored sugar. Decorate with crystallized fruit or gummy bears.

How to Make a Sugar Skull

Sugar skulls are brightly colored candies shaped like skulls. People often eat them, just like valentine candy. They remind us that we, too, will die someday. This is not morbid or sad. Instead, it is a reminder to enjoy life while we're here.

Ingredients:
2 cups sifted powdered sugar
1 egg white
1 tablespoon light corn syrup
½ teaspoon of vanilla
⅓ cup of corn starch
food coloring
1 fine paintbrush

Preparation: Mix egg white, syrup and vanilla in a dry bowl. Mix the sifted powdered sugar into the mixture gradually with your fingers until it forms a ball. Sprinkle cornstarch on a table or cutting board. Place the mixture on the table and shape it into a smooth ball. Wrap tightly in plastic and chill until ready to use. (It will keep for several months.)

When you make it into skulls and other shapes, use molds, which you can purchase online or in Mexican stores. If you don't have molds, use plenty of corn starch.

When the figures have dried, use the food coloring and fine paintbrush to color them the way you want.

ARE flowers carried to the kingdom of death?

Is it true that we go? Is it true that we go?

Where do we go? Where do we go?

Are we dead there or do we still live?

Do we exist there again?

—LINES FROM AN ANCIENT NAHUATL POEM

Other Bilingual Books for Kids from Cinco Puntos Press

Cada Niño / Every Child
A Bilingual Songbook for Kids
By Tish Hinojosa
Illustrated by Lucia Angela Perez

Pájaro Verde / The Green Bird
As told by Joe Hayes
Illustrated by Antonio Castro L.

¡El Cucuy! A Bogeyman Cuento
in English and Spanish
As told by Joe Hayes
Illustrated by Honorio Robledo

El Ratoncito Pequeño / The Little Mouse
A Nursery Rhyme in Spanish and English
Remembered by Pipina Salas-Porras
Illustrated by José Cisneros

Grandma Fina and Her Wonderful Umbrellas
La Abuelita Fina y Sus Sombrillas Maravillosas
By Benjamin Alire Saenz
Illustrated by Geronimo Garcia

La Llorona / The Weeping Woman
As told by Joe Hayes
Illustrated by Vicki Trego Hill

Tell Me a Cuento / Cuéntame un Story
4 Stories in English & Spanish
As told by Joe Hayes
Illustrated by Geronimo Garcia

Cinco Puntos Press

Our complete catalog is online.
www.cincopuntos.com
or call 1-800-566-9072